Let's Celebrate

Christmas

CRAFTS, RECIPES, STORIES, AND ACTIVITIES TO SHARE

HIGHLIGHTS PRESS

A HIGHLIGHTS COMPANY

Honesdale, Pennsylvania

Copyright © 2012 by Highlights Press
A division of Highlights for Children, Inc.
Cover illustration by Mary Sullivan
All rights reserved

Some selections in this book first appeared in *Highlights High Five*™
magazine and *Fun-to-Make Crafts for Christmas* (Boyds Mills
Press) and are used or adapted with permission.

For information about permission to reproduce selections from this
book, please contact permissions@highlights.com.

Published by Highlights Press
A division of Highlights for Children, Inc.
815 Church Street
Honesdale, Pennsylvania 18431

Printed in the United States of America

ISBN: 978-1-59078-967-4
Library of Congress Control Number: 2012941726

First edition
Visit our website at highlights.com.
10 9 8 7 6 5 4 3 2 1

Christmas is a magical time! To get ready for the holiday, families decorate the house and trim the tree, stir up favorite treats and make cards and gifts. *Let's Celebrate Christmas* shows you how to create traditions that will help make the holiday special. With simple crafts and recipes, read-aloud stories and poems, and fun-to-do puzzles and activities, it's perfect for sharing with young children. But there's something for everyone to enjoy.

CONTENTS

Little Bunny's Christmas Sled

by Eileen Spinelli

Illustrated by Rose Mary Berlin

Little Bunny got a new red sled for Christmas. He couldn't wait to use it! Luckily, the very next morning Little Bunny woke to snow.

He had a quick breakfast.
He bundled up and got his
sled. Then he went to his friend
Squirrel's house.

"Grab your sled," said Little Bunny. "We'll go to Holly
Jolly Hill."

Squirrel sighed. "My sled broke the last time I used it."

"That's too bad," said Little Bunny. He thought: I will be
extra careful with my sled.

Little Bunny went to Holly Jolly Hill by himself. He coasted down. By himself. He pulled his sled up the hill again. By himself.

He thought: Sledding by myself is not as much fun as sledding with Squirrel. He thought: Squirrel and I could take turns on my sled. And then he thought: But what if Squirrel breaks my sled?

Little Bunny remembered what Mama had said when he accidentally broke her striped vase. "It's only a vase, after all."

"It's only a sled, after all," said Little Bunny. And off he went to get Squirrel.

Little Bunny and Squirrel took turns going up and down Holly Jolly Hill. They swooped and whooped. They tumbled and laughed.

When it was time to go, Squirrel noticed a scratch on Little Bunny's sled. "Oh no!" he said.

Little Bunny smiled. "It's only a scratch, after all," he said. "Sledding with you is the best Christmas present ever. Let's go again tomorrow."

And that's exactly what they did.

9

Sharing Christmas

ILLUSTRATED BY CAROL THOMPSON

For Christmas I'd like to . . .

share popcorn and a movie with you.

For Christmas I'd like to . . .

visit a museum with you.

For Christmas I'd like to . . .

build a snow castle with you.

For Christmas I'd like to . . .

bake cupcakes with you.

For Christmas I'd like to . . .

have a playdate with you.

For Christmas I'd like to . . .

take a train ride with you.

For Christmas I'd like to . . .

sing songs with you and my friends.

For Christmas I'd like to . . .

give you lots of hugs and kisses.

Christmas is a good time to do special things with family and friends. And it's a good time to let them know how much you like being with them. You can do that with a Christmas card. Fold a piece of sturdy white paper in half. Think about someone you'd like to spend time with. Imagine what you would do together. On the front of the card, draw a picture of what you imagined. On the inside, write the words "For Christmas I'd like to . . ." and then finish the sentence. Give your Christmas card to that special person.
Adult: Help with the writing as needed.

MY FIRST Hidden Pictures™

PUZZLE

ILLUSTRATED BY ELLEN APPLEBY

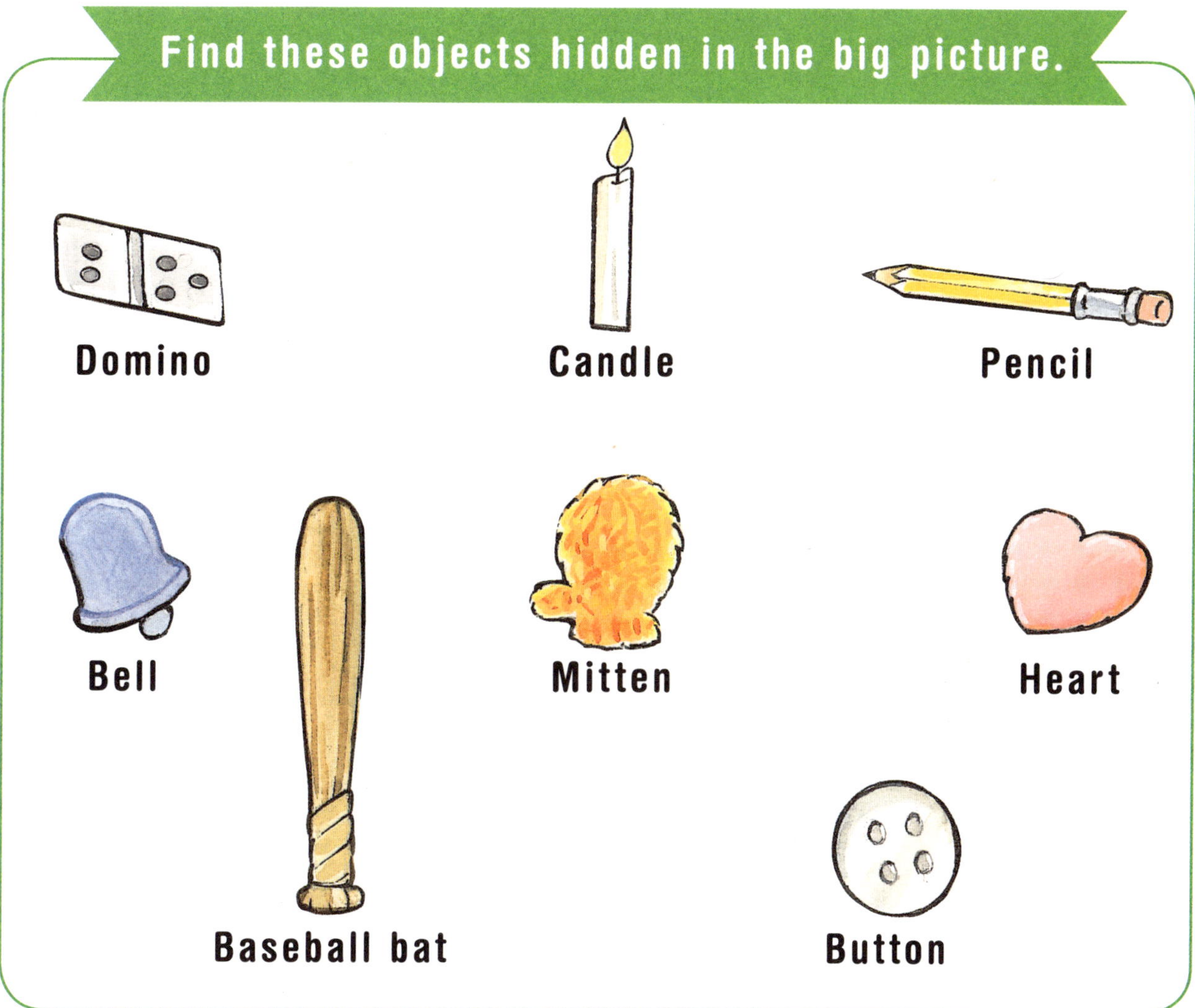

Little Jack Horner

Little Jack Horner

Sat in a corner,

Eating a Christmas pie.

He put in his thumb,

And pulled out a plum,

And said, "What a good boy am I!"

Gingerbread

ILLUSTRATED BY AMANDA HALEY

YOU WILL NEED:

3 eggs	2 teaspoons baking soda	**Adult**: Preheat oven to 350 degrees. Lightly grease a 12" x 14" baking pan with vegetable oil.
1 cup corn oil	1 teaspoon allspice	
1 cup molasses	1 teaspoon cinnamon	
1 cup sugar	1 teaspoon ginger	
2 cups flour	1 cup boiling water	

1   **2**   **3**

Directions

1. Place eggs, oil, molasses, and sugar in a large bowl and mix well.

2. In another bowl, mix flour, baking soda, and spices.

3. Add dry ingredients to wet ingredients. Mix well.

Adult: Add boiling water. Fold into batter. Pour batter into pan and bake 45 minutes. Cool and serve.

Meringue Snowmen

BY MARY MULARD
ILLUSTRATED BY AMANDA HALEY

YOU WILL NEED:

2 eggs (whites only)
pinch of salt
½ cup sugar

currants, dried cranberries,
or mini chocolate chips

Adult: Preheat oven to 200 degrees. Lightly coat a cookie sheet with vegetable oil.

Directions

1. **Adult**: Separate eggs, placing whites in a mixing bowl. Add a pinch of salt and beat until fluffy. Gradually add sugar until firm peaks form.

2. Make a snowman shape by dropping 3 spoonfuls of meringue onto the cookie sheet. Use the back of the spoon to smooth the meringue.

3. Decorate with currants, dried cranberries, or mini chocolate chips.

Adult: Bake snowmen for 2 hours, until lightly browned. Cool and serve. Store any leftovers in an airtight container.

Thumbprint Cookies

BY HEIDE WELNER
ILLUSTRATED BY AMANDA HALEY

YOU WILL NEED:

2 sticks butter at room
  temperature

¾ cup brown sugar

½ teaspoon vanilla

2 eggs, separated

2 cups flour

½ teaspoon salt

1 cup ground almonds or
  pecans

½ cup seedless raspberry jam

Adult: Preheat oven to
375 degrees and cover a
baking sheet with foil.

Directions

1. Adult: Cream together
butter, sugar, and vanilla.
Add egg yolks one at a
time. (Reserve whites.)

2. Mix together flour
and salt. Slowly add to
creamed mixture. Dough
will be stiff.

3. Add 2 tablespoons
water to egg whites. Mix
well and pour into a flat
bowl. Place ground nuts in
a separate flat bowl.

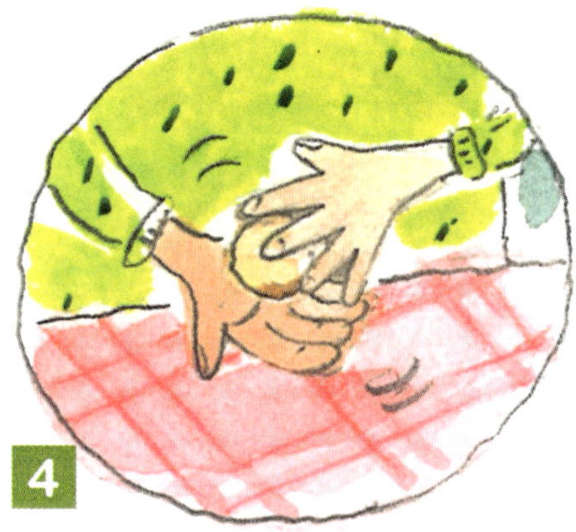

4. Roll a clump of dough so it makes a ball about 1 inch across.

5. Roll it in the egg whites and then in the ground nuts till covered.

6. Place the ball on a baking sheet and flatten slightly. Use your thumb to make a deep indent in the center. Repeat until all the dough is used up.

7. Adult: Bake cookies for about 10 minutes, or until golden brown. Slide foil with cookies onto a rack and let cool completely. Fill each thumbprint with jam. Makes 4 dozen cookies.

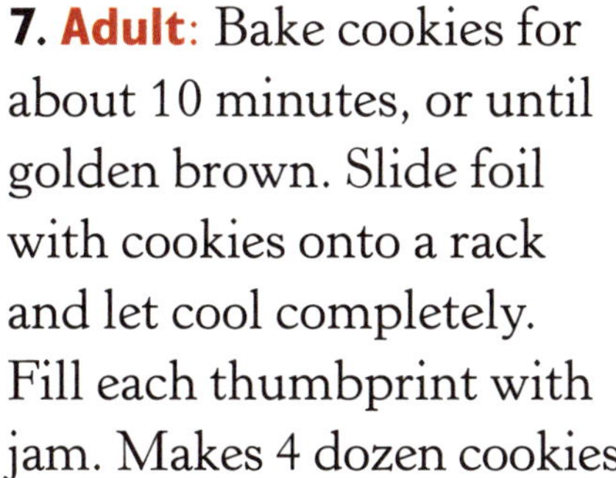

Pinecone Decorations

Christmas Candleholders

YOU WILL NEED: old CD, small wooden candleholder, pinecones, small ornaments, paintbrush, white glue; optional: silver or white glitter

Directions

1. Turn the CD facedown and glue the wooden candleholder to its center.

2. Arrange the pinecones around the candleholder. Glue them in place. Then glue small ornaments in the empty spaces.

3. If you like, brush white glue on the tips of the pinecones and sprinkle on glitter. Let dry, then place a candle in the holder.

Winter Tree

1

2

3

Directions

1. Attach 2 star stickers to the top of the pinecone so that they stick together with the tip of the cone between them.

2. Dab some glue on the pinecone and put decorations in place. You can use tweezers to help with this step.

3. Turn the plate upside down. Pull apart cotton balls so they lose their shape. Mound them on the plate. Then place the pinecone Christmas tree in the center of the mound.

Christmas Tree Decorations

ILLUSTRATED BY CHRIS CASE

Cinnamon-Scented Ornaments

YOU WILL NEED: ½ cup cinnamon*, ½ cup smooth applesauce, waxed paper, cookie cutters, plastic straw, ribbon or yarn

*For gingerbread-scented ornaments, substitute nutmeg and allspice for some of the cinnamon.

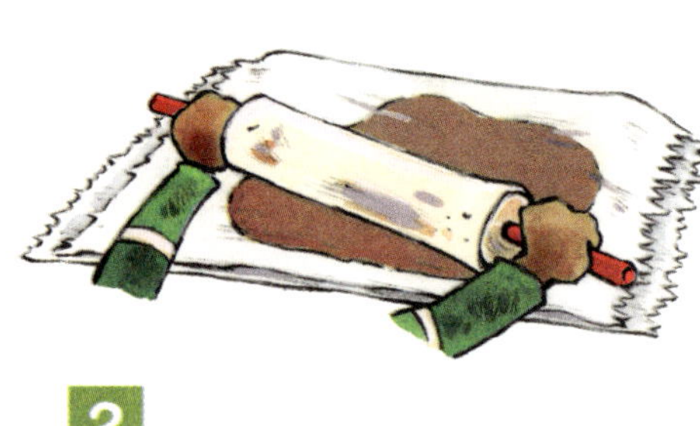

Directions

1. In bowl, mix together cinnamon and applesauce to make dough. Knead it a bit. If it's too sticky to handle, add more cinnamon. If it's too dry to hold together, add more applesauce.

2. Place dough between 2 pieces of waxed paper. Using a rolling pin, flatten dough till it's about ¼ inch thick.

3. Use cookie cutters to cut dough into shapes. Then use a straw to poke a hole at the top of each shape.

4. Place ornaments on paper plates. Let dry 5–7 days, turning over regularly. Thread a piece of ribbon or yarn through each hole and tie in a loop.

Patchwork Ornaments

1

2

3

Directions

1. Trace around cookie cutters on foam paper. Then cut out shapes.

2. Glue small patches of fabric onto shapes until they're completely covered. **Adult:** Trim any excess fabric from edges as needed. Then poke a hole at the top of the ornament.

3. When glue is dry, thread a piece of ribbon or yarn through each hole and tie in a loop.

Soup to Share

SUPPLIES: Christmas wrapping paper or colorful fabric, ribbon, pinking scissors, glue, wide-mouth 1-pint (2 cup) jar

INGREDIENTS:

1 teaspoon salt	1 tablespoon dried minced onion	½ cup red lentils
¼ teaspoon lemon pepper		½ cup brown rice
1 tablespoon dried parsley	½ cup split green peas	
1 bay leaf	½ cup barley	

Directions

1. Cut circle of fabric or wrapping paper 3 inches wider than lid of jar.

2. Put glue on top of lid. Center fabric or paper on lid and press down. Let dry.

3. Put first 5 ingredients into jar. Then pour in other ingredients, one at a time, to make layers.

4. Put lid on jar and smooth paper or fabric over sides. Tie on a ribbon.
Adult: Copy recipe card on page 29 and attach to jar.

Give as a gift to say Merry Christmas!

Soup to Share

1. Pour the contents of this jar into a big pot. Add 6 cups of your favorite broth.

2. Add 1 cup of chopped celery and 1 cup of chopped carrot to the pot.

3. Bring to a boil. Then simmer, covered, until all ingredients are tender (about one hour).

4. Before serving, add one 14.5-ounce can of chopped tomatoes, including liquid.

That's Silly!

ILLUSTRATED BY PAULA BECKER

WELCOME TO THE NORTH POLE
Santa's elves are busy! What silly things do you see?

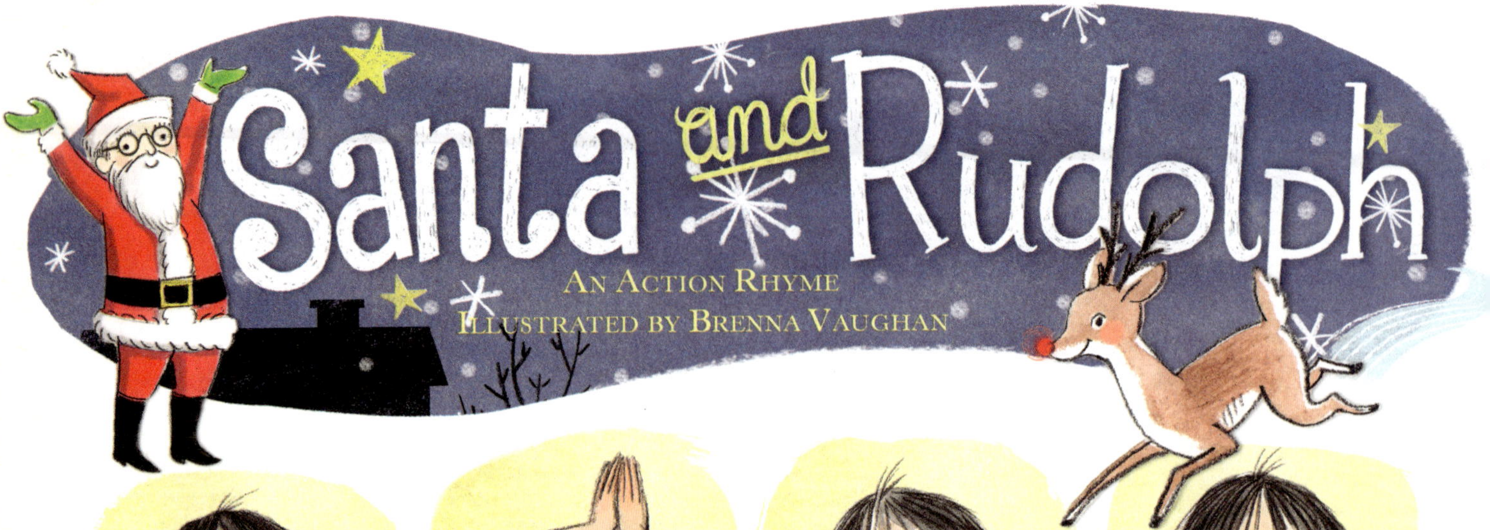

Santa and Rudolph

An Action Rhyme

Illustrated by Brenna Vaughan

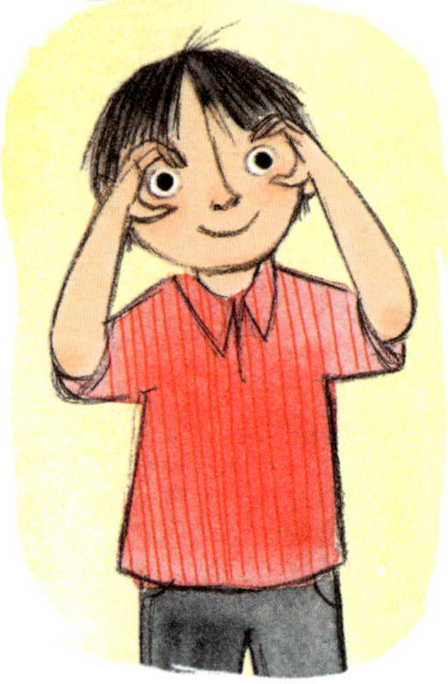

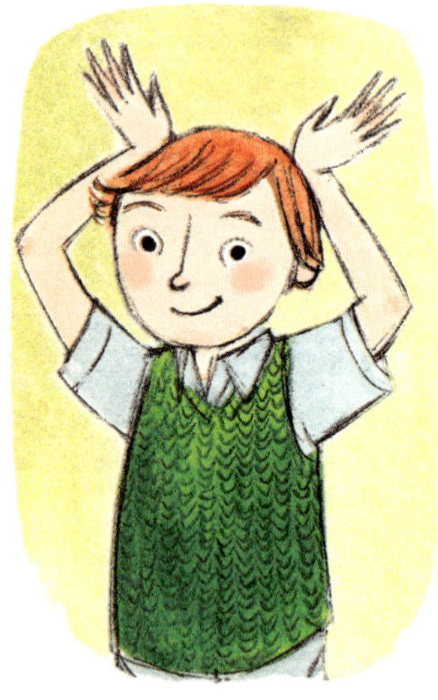

Here are
Santa's glasses.

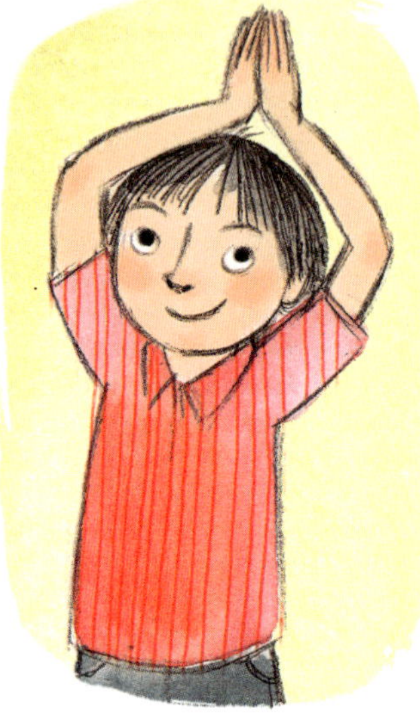

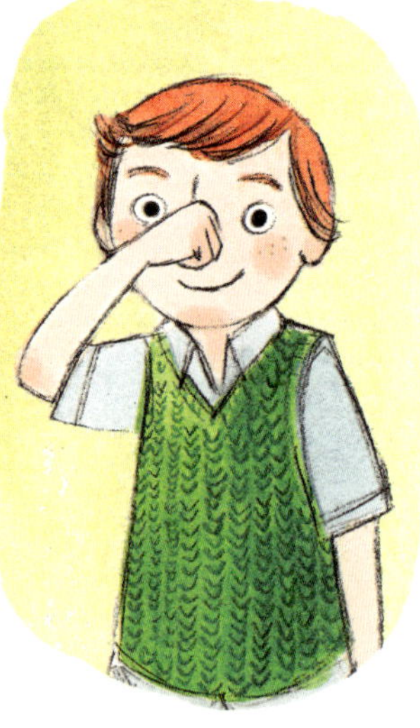

And here is
Santa's cap.

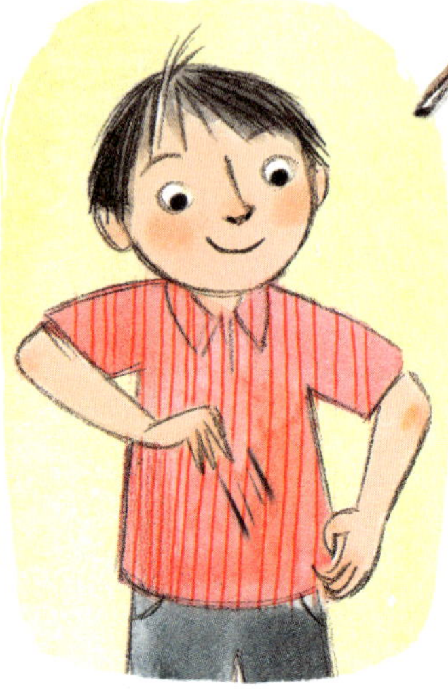

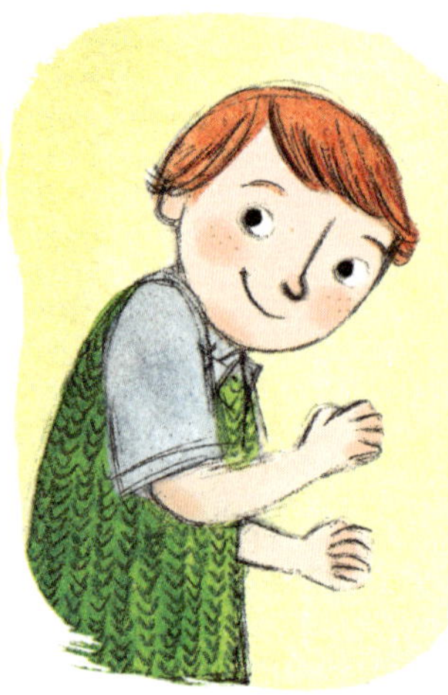

And here's
the way he
fills his bag

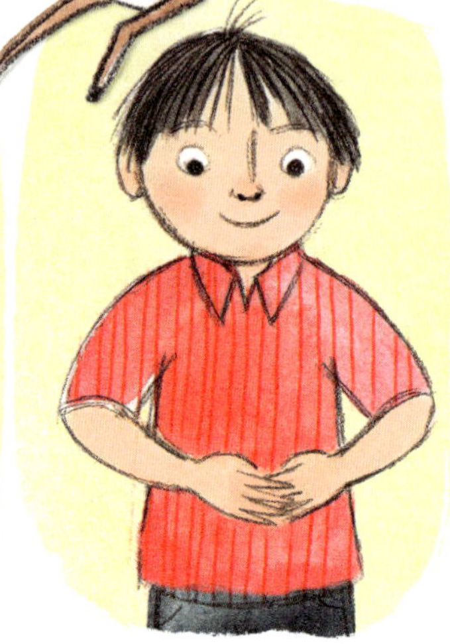

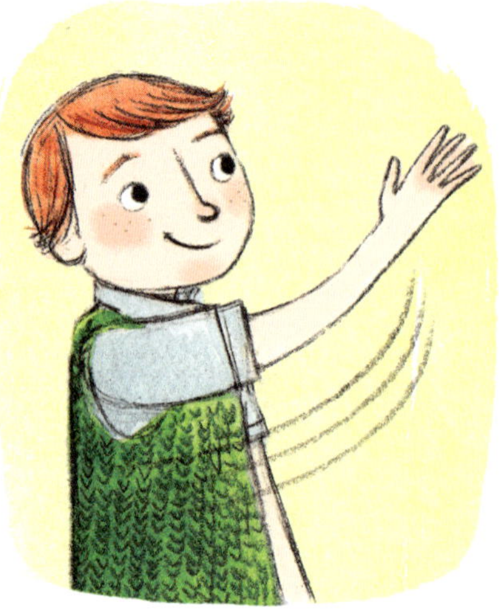

and puts it
in his lap.

Here are
Rudolph's
antlers.

And here is
Rudolph's
nose.

And here's
the way he
pulls the sleigh

as through
the sky it goes!